Christmas Magic

Sue Stainton

ILLUSTRATED BY
Eva Melhuish

KATHERINE TEGEN BOOKS ❄ *An Imprint of* HarperCollins*Publishers*

Christmas Magic
Text copyright © 2007 by Sue Stainton
Illustrations copyright © 2007 by Eva Melhuish

Manufactured in China.
For information address HarperCollins Children's Books, a division of HarperCollins Publishers,
1350 Avenue of the Americas, New York, NY 10019.
www.harpercollinschildrens.com
Library of Congress Cataloging-in-Publication Data is available.
ISBN-10: 0-06-078571-3 (trade bdg.) — ISBN-13: 978-0-06-078571-0 (trade bdg.)
ISBN-10: 0-06-078572-1 (lib. bdg.) — ISBN-13: 978-0-06-078572-7 (lib. bdg.)
Typography by Carla Weise 1 2 3 4 5 6 7 8 9 10 ❖ First Edition

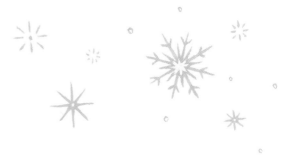

To Thomas and Rachel,
Michael and Amelia
—S.S.

To Charlie and Zoë
and a special thank-you
to Little Santa—Tomten
—E.M.

*L*ittle Santa looks after the forest.
He knows all the animals and trees by name.

Once a year he plans a special treat for his friends. Little Santa is full of surprises.

Everyone waits and wonders.
Is something about to happen?

Suddenly the reindeer realize their bells are missing.
And the whole forest is whispering
because the bells are full of Christmas magic.

The trees whisper to the animals.
Where could the bells be?
We will have a treasure hunt to find them!

The animals all look for clues.

They look up.

They look down.

They play hide-and-seek.

They see footprints and follow.
Is someone there?

Was that music or
the trees laughing?
Reindeer looks
everywhere.
Ting-a-ling.
A reindeer bell!

Was that jingling,
or was it the wind?
Something taps Rabbit
on the head.
OUCH!
A reindeer bell!

Was that the snow singing?
Squirrel listens.
Scrabble, scrabble, dig.
A reindeer bell!

What was going around and around?
Squirrel is chasing a musical tail!

A
reindeer
bell!

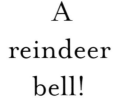

Who was playing circus tricks?

Mouse is balancing on
something that rolls and tinkles.
Another reindeer bell!

Everyone is playing tricks now—
they're all playing tricks on one another.

BOO!

HA,HA!

But where are the other missing magical bells? *Where?*

Suddenly, in the distance, they hear something.
Ssshhh!

The animals play follow-the-leader
toward the noise.

Deeper into the forest they go.
All is quiet, all is black. They are lost.

They have not gone this far into the forest before. Ever.
The trees seem to close in behind them. Silence.

They are really frightened now.
Then suddenly, around a corner,

the moon comes out.
Surprise!

The largest of the forest trees bows.
It is all dressed up. Icicles tinkle, ice stars twinkle.
The missing magical reindeer bells jingle and
scatter Christmas magic everywhere.

Music fills the forest.

Little Santa jumps out and claps at the concert.

He does a cartwheel in the snow.

And Santa throws Christmas magic into the sky.
It sparkles all around.

Everyone is laughing. Everyone is dancing.

Suddenly the night sky
is alight with shooting stars.

And midnight moonbeams
light up the forest.

"A magical Christmas to you all!"

Little Santa laughs as he jingles the last reindeer
bell in his pocket, keeping the last of the
Christmas magic safe—*for next year.*